CANDICE F. RANSOM

When the Whippoorwill Calls

pictures by KIMBERLY BULCKEN ROOT

TAMBOURINE BOOKS  NEW YORK

LIBRARY OF CONGRESS CATALOGING IN PUBLICATION DATA
Ransom, Candice F., 1952– When the whippoorwill calls / by Candice F.
Ransom; pictures by Kimberly Bulcken Root. — 1st ed. p. cm. Summary:
A Blue Ridge Mountain family is displaced to the flatlands by the creation of the Shenandoah
National Park. 1. Shenandoah National Park (Va.)—Fiction.
[1. Mountain life—Virginia—Fiction. 2. Blue Ridge Mountains—Fiction.
3. Virginia—Fiction. 4. Moving, Household—Fiction.] I. Root, Kimberly Bulcken, ill.
II. Title. PZ7.R1743Wg 1995 [E]—dc20 94-41567 CIP AC
ISBN 0-688-12729-0 (TR). — ISBN 0-688-12730-4 (LE)
1 3 5 7 9 10 8 6 4 2
First edition

*For Frank, who shared the wonders of
Shenandoah National Park with me*
C.F.R.

For Janna and Opal and Olive
K.B.R.

Every seven years, the peak of our mountain
glowed with yellow fire.
Pap told me that story
the summer I was seven.

"The mountain is filled with gold," he said.
"And the glow will lead you to the treasure."
"Can we go find the gold?" I asked.
Pap laughed. "That's fool-talk.
Like that tale about the government
buying the mountain for the park."
I laughed too. Nobody could buy a mountain!

In the woods we heard
Whip-whip-*whip*-poor-will!
"The first whippoorwill," Pap said.
"Turn a somersault and make a wish."
I tried to somersault but tumbled
in the soft clover of the apple orchard,
my legs sprawled every which way.

Back then we lived in a holler so deep,
shadows made it seem like twilight all the time.
Every morning I helped Pap tote water from the well.
In the evenings Mama lit the coal-oil lamps
and took up lapfuls of mending
while I did my sums.

Mr. Spitler owned the land we lived on.
We looked after his cattle in return.
Mr. Spitler's family had owned this land a long time.
Just as *our* family had lived on this land a long time.
Mr. Spitler's place probably had inside taps
and electric lights.
But I bet there weren't any whippoorwills.

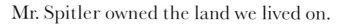

The summer I turned seven,
Mama and I picked buckets of huckleberries
from the bushes drowsing in the sun.
I looked for the glow, but saw no sign of it.
Mama made jam, rows and rows of jars
that went *snap-pop* as they set.

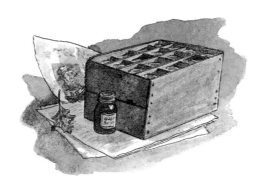

Pap packed Mama's jam in the wagon.
We were all going over the mountain to the store.
We left before daybreak.
As we crested the top, I watched the stars fall
around my daddy's head.
Far off I saw the shimmer of light.
"Is it the treasure?" I whispered.
"You might say," Pap answered.
"That light marks the beginning of a new day."

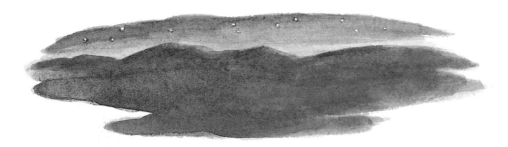

At the store, old men tilted back
in hickory-bottomed rockers,
gossiping about the coming of the park.
"Just so the city people
can enjoy our scenery!" Pap scoffed.

People would have picnics on our mountain,
fish in our stream, trample our huckleberry thickets.
Yet all up and down the Blue Ridge,
folks were selling their land.
Bit by bit, the park was taking our mountain.

The snows came, and
Pap wove white oak strips into baskets.
Century baskets, he called them.
That's how long they'd last.
Pap would sing "Pretty Polly" while he worked.
I thought he made up that song just for me
because my name is Polly too.

Pap strung the baskets along his back and arms.
Turtlelike, he'd hike over the mountain
to sell the jag of baskets at the store.
I walked to school in knee-high snowdrifts
and thought our life on the mountain
would last forever, like Pap's baskets.

Then one day Pap told us Mr. Spitler had sold our land.

"We'll have to move," he said.

Move! Leave the mountain that was our home?

"Where will we live?" Mama asked.

"The government is building us a new house," Pap replied.

"Down below in the Flatlands." His voice was dull.

How could we live down below?

We belonged in the hills.

But like it or not, the park was coming.

Mama washed all our clothes
and draped them to dry on bushes.
Pap hammered boxes to put our canning jars in.

I hunted for a glimmer of yellow.
If only I could find the gold!
Then *we* could buy the whole mountain.
But the mountain would not give up its secret.

It was time to leave.
Shadows closed over our cabin
as we slowly climbed the mountain
one last time.

We made our way down to the valley.

The open fields and scattered trees bothered my eyes.

But our new house was a glory,

white-painted, with inside taps and electric lights.

Mama flipped the switch on and off,

her face lit with amazement.

From the kitchen window we could see our mountain.

It looked distant and strange from down here.

That winter, Pap sat by the stove, making baskets.

I asked him to sing "Pretty Polly."

He sang, but his heart wasn't in it.

Now he had a truck to carry his baskets.
I rode a golden bus to my new school.
Mama pinned our washing to a spun-silver clothesline.
Though I missed our cabin in the holler,
the new house was nice too.

When spring came, Pap plowed a garden.
Every now and then I caught him
glancing up at the mountain,
as if he'd left something there.

One day he said, "Let's you and me walk
yonder up the mountain."
The park men were bulldozing a new road.
Trees lay across the creek like fallen soldiers.
"It's all different," I said sadly.

Pap didn't speak.
We slipped down the overgrown path
to our holler.

I was afraid our old place would be gone,
but it was still there.
Wisteria swagged over the cabin doorway.
Briars snagged my legs as I ran through
our apple orchard.

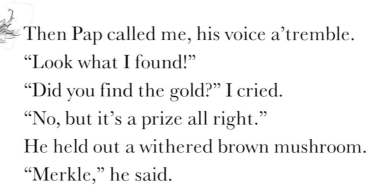

Then Pap called me, his voice a'tremble.
"Look what I found!"
"Did you find the gold?" I cried.
"No, but it's a prize all right."
He held out a withered brown mushroom.
"Merkle," he said.

For an instant I thought he said "Miracle."
"Merkles are a rare treat," Pap added.
"They only grow in abandoned orchards.
Wait'll you taste them!"

We gathered mushrooms like they were gold pieces.
Pap hummed "Pretty Polly" as he filled his sack.
"We'll come back every year," he vowed.
"It won't be the same," I said.
Pap's hands cupped a tiny merkle,
the mountain's secret treasure.
"Sometimes," he said, "change is good."

From deep in the woods came
Whip-whip-*whip*-poor-will!
I turned a perfect somersault.
Pap laughed and told me to make a wish.
But my wish had already come true.
For a little while,
the mountain was ours again.

Halfway down the trail, we spied the warm
glow of yellow fire . . .
our little house below, bright as a new day.

Mama had put on every light,
welcoming us home.

AUTHOR'S NOTE

The Blue Ridge Mountains of Virginia first attracted settlers over two hundred years ago. People moved into the hollows between the mountains. They cut down trees and burned off acres, turning the wilderness into farmland.

In 1924, a portion of the Blue Ridge was chosen as the site for a national park near the nation's capital. Some 465 families lived within park boundaries. Most of these families did not own the land they lived on and farmed. The landowners sold their property, so the mountain families had to move.

Homesteads were built in neighboring valleys. Many moved into these houses; others bought land elsewhere. A few elderly residents were permitted to stay in their mountain homes the rest of their lives.

In July 1936, President Franklin D. Roosevelt dedicated the Shenandoah National Park, an eighty-mile length of woods and streams everyone can enjoy. Nature gradually took back the farmland and pastures. The Blue Ridge Mountains are wild and beautiful again.

The homes of the mountain people were torn down or allowed to decay. But there are signs that people once lived in the hollows.

If you wander off one of the trails, you might come across a tottering stone chimney or a rock wall. And if you close your eyes, you might hear the *snap-pop* of jam jars or someone humming "Pretty Polly."